# FLOWER GARDEN

WRITTEN BY

## Eve Bunting

ILLUSTRATED BY

## Kathryn Hewitt

SCHOLASTIC INC.

New York  Toronto  London  Auckland  Sydney
Mexico City  New Delhi  Hong Kong

ISBN 0-439-19571-3

Text copyright © 1994 by Eve Bunting.
Illustrations copyright © 1994 by Kathryn Hewitt.
All rights reserved.
Published by Scholastic Inc., 555 Broadway,
New York, NY 10012, by arrangement with
Harcourt Brace & Co., Inc.
SCHOLASTIC and associated logos are trademarks and/or
registered trademarks of Scholastic Inc.

12 11 10 9 8 7 6 5 4 3 2 1     0 1 2 3 4 5/0

Printed in the U.S.A.          09

The paintings in this book were done in oil paint on paper.
The display type and text type were set in Benguiat.
Designed by Lisa Peters.

*For Anna Eve,*
*who makes beautiful flower gardens.*

*— E. B.*

*For Diane D'Andrade and Jeannette Larson,*
*who can turn dandelions into daffodils.*

*— K. H.*

Garden in a shopping cart
Doesn't it look great?

Garden on the checkout stand
I can hardly wait.

Garden in a cardboard box
Walking to the bus

Garden sitting on our laps
People smile at us!

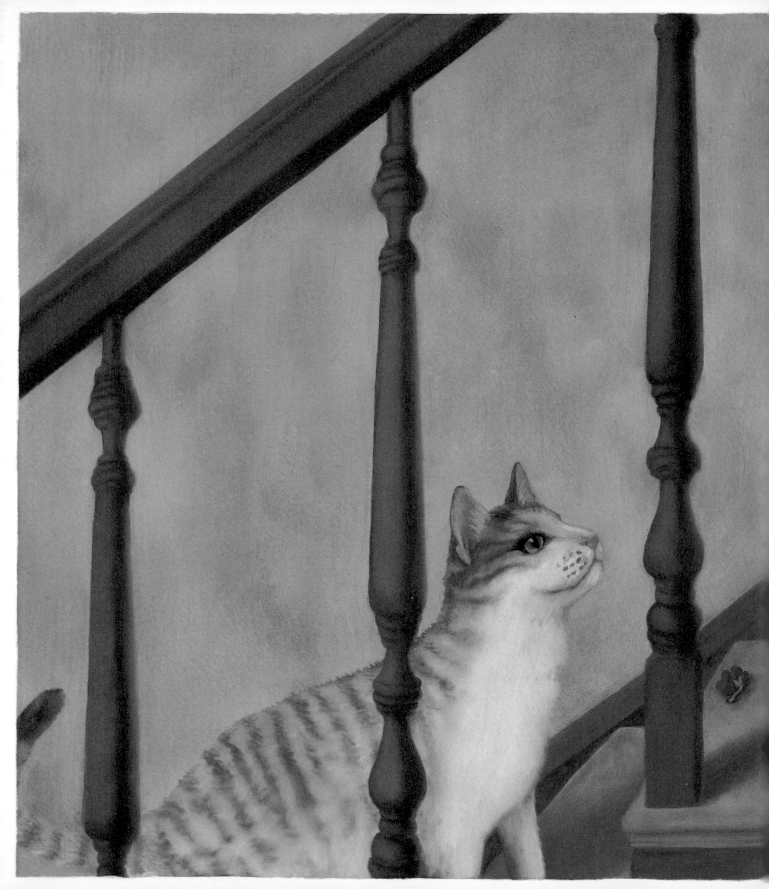

Garden going up the stairs
Stopping at each floor

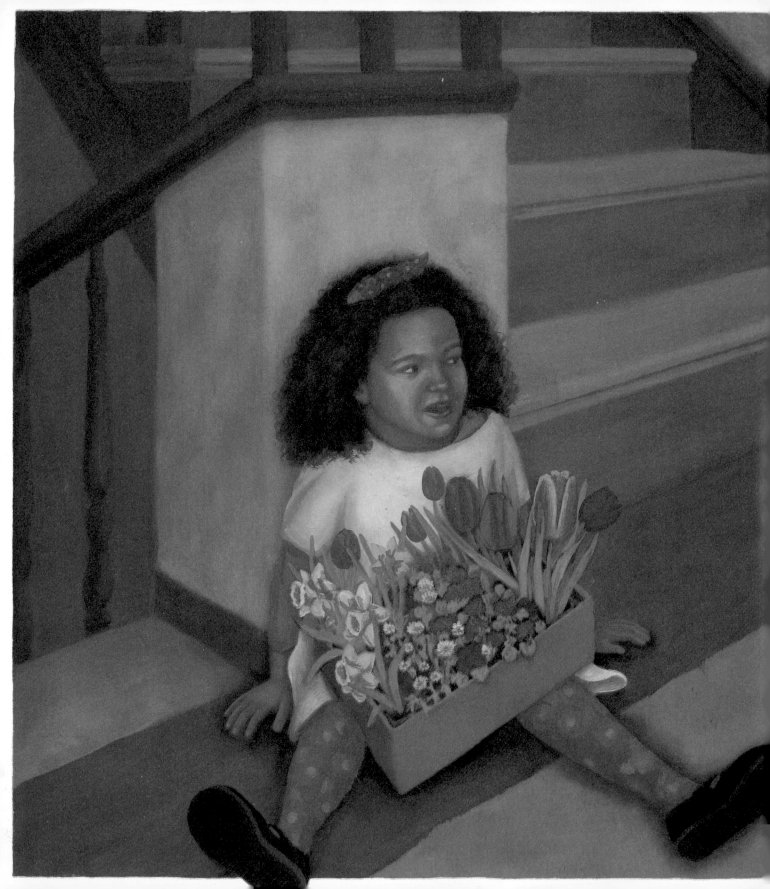

This garden's getting heavier!
At last — our own front door.

Hurry! Hurry! Get the trowel
Spread the papers thick.

Get the bag of potting soil
Get the planting mix.

Put purple
pansies at
each end

Daisies, white
as snow

Daffodils, geraniums

and tulips in a row.

Garden in a window box
High above the street

Where butterflies
can stop and rest
And ladybugs can meet.

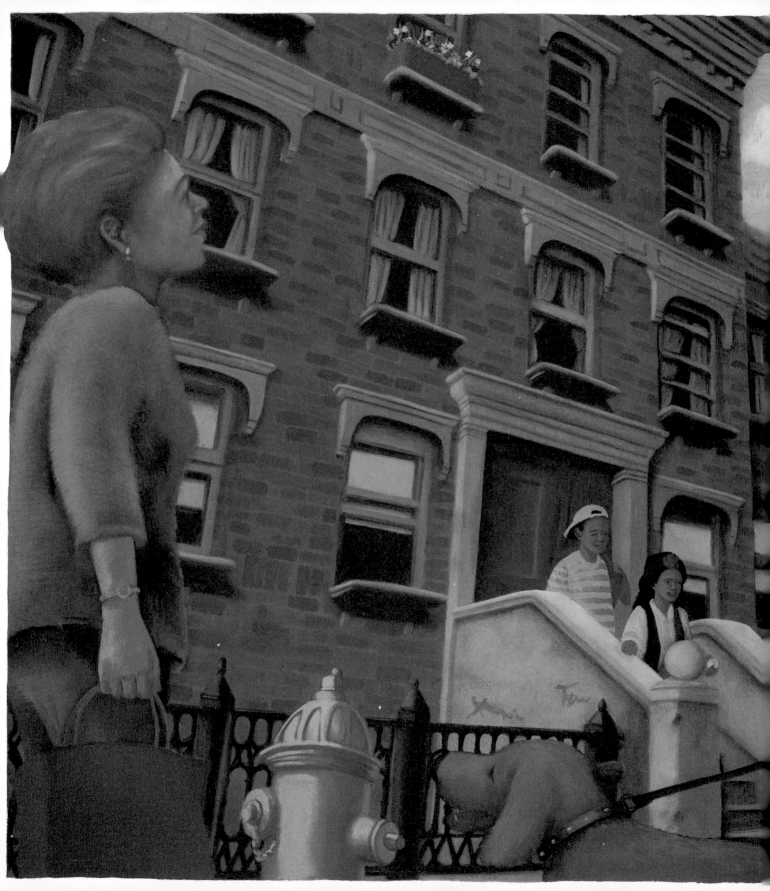

Walkers walking down below
Will lift their heads and see
Purple, yellow, red, and white
A color jamboree.

Candles on a birthday cake
Chocolate ice cream, too.

Happy, happy birthday, Mom!
A garden box — for you.